Check ou

S

Scien

How far would you go to break into
the movies? Get the answer in
BEHIND THE SCREAMS

It's alive. It's growing. It's *hungry*. See why in
BZZZZ

Earth is in for a big jolt. Check out why in
SHORT CIRCUIT

There's a whole lot of shakin' going on!
Read all about it in
SUPER STAR

What *are* those robots talking about?
Find out in
THE LOST LANGUAGE

All that glitters isn't good! See why in
CHARMERS

History can really get to you! Learn more in
BLAST FROM THE PAST

You may get more than you bargained for!
Check out
COSMIC EXCHANGE

This fan is out of this world!
Find out why in
ALIEN OBSESSION

ISBN 0-8114-9321-0

9 10 07 06 05

Produced by Mega-Books of New York, Inc.
Design and Art Direction by Michaelis/Carpelis Design Assoc.

Cover illustration: Wayne Alfano

WARP WORLD 3030

by T. M. West

interior illustrations by
Freya Tanz

www.steck-vaughn.com

CHAPTER 1

Hobie Negron carefully made his way across the dangerous landscape of Valhalla 7. The atmosphere of the unfriendly planet was hot and sticky.

An expert explorer, Hobie doubted anything lived on this land of jagged stones. Nothing but the pillars that grew out of Valhalla 7's clay soil could be seen across the flat plane of this strange planet.

Hobie's legs ached from hiking over the stone ruins, and he began to consider calling off his assignment.

He stopped to rest in the shadows between two of the stone pillars.

Suddenly, a hissing sound came out from the darkness from behind him.

Hobie turned to face two space Cobrans. The creatures were man-sized beasts with the heads of cobras and humanoid bodies. Hobie knew full well the danger he was in. The venom of a Cobran could kill a man in less than a minute.

"Huuuman," one of the monsters cackled, "you ssshhhould not have come here!"

The Cobrans began to advance on Hobie, bearing their fangs. Their forked tongues danced hungrily from side to side.

"You ssshhhall be our prey!" the other creature said with a sneer.

Hobie began to back up. The Cobrans continued toward him. Their grey, scaly forms moved quickly along the stones.

"I am Hobie Negron, a professional explorer from the Midgard II," Hobie

announced to the creatures.

He reached for the weapon hanging from his belt and rested his hand there. "I come in peace," he added.

"Ahh, but we don't," one of the creatures replied. It raised its huge back legs to pounce.

Hobie quickly drew his weapon and

fired. The first Cobran shrieked as the ray lifted it from the ground and slammed it against the stone. The creature slumped to the soil. The Cobran was knocked out.

"Hobie," a voice called. "It's time for lunch! Come on down."

As the second Cobran launched into the air, its glistening fangs descending upon him, Hobie shrugged.

"Freeze program," Hobie said softly. The monster froze in mid-air.

"Save ninth level of Valhalla 7 for completion," Hobie said. He finished playing the virtual reality game. Hobie took off his helmet and gloves. Then he stepped off the digital treadmill that adjusted its pitch to the computer program's landscape.

Hobie walked into the dining room where his mother, Dr. Carmen Negron, was putting two plates of food on the dining room table. Carmen was the head science officer for the Midgard II. She was home for her lunch hour.

"Do you have enough time to eat before you battle any more space creatures?" Hobie's mother asked with a friendly grin.

"I think I could adjust my schedule for lunch," Hobie replied, licking his lips. He sat down at the table.

"That's good," Carmen said, sitting next to Hobie as he ate. "And please don't spend all day on that game. There are more interesting things you could be doing."

"You know, if I had a Skyye, I wouldn't need to play virtual reality games," Hobie said.

"Hobie, we've discussed this before," Carmen said evenly. "After what happened to your brother in that red zone warp world, your father and I don't think you're ready for a Skyye."

"Mom, why are you holding what

happened to Jack against me?" Hobie protested. "He was a professional explorer. I'm just a social misfit who wants to have some fun. Everyone my age has a Skyye."

"We can discuss it again when your father comes home. That should be in about an hour," Carmen replied.

"Okay," Hobie gave in. "That gives me

enough time to digest my lunch then go for a jog."

"Sure," Carmen replied. "Be back by one if you want to talk to your father."

"You got it," Hobie agreed, wisking his dishes into the kitchen.

After letting his lunch settle, Hobie slipped into his running shoes and went outside for a jog down the quiet

sidewalk. There was no one else around.

Hobie and his family lived on the Midgard II. The Midgard II looked like a planet, but was actually a huge, moving research space station that scanned space for new life-forms and planets. Hobie had lived all of his sixteen years on Midgard II.

Hobie jogged down the sidewalk of his block, which looked like any Earth neighborhood. He admired the green grass and the lush trees that were created by the Midgard II. The Midgard II made its own seasons under the invisible field that surrounded the space station.

Hobie thought about the sun on the unexplored edge of the galaxy the Midgard II was currently orbiting. The giant station had been monitoring different regions of this sector of the galaxy for six years.

While Dr. Carmen Negron was the

head science officer for the station, Hobie's father, Ernie "Space Ace" Negron, was its commander. Ernie was famous for being a top-notch space pilot. Hobie hoped to be joining his father as an explorer of the galaxy, commonly known as the New Frontier, as soon as he was old enough to train.

Hobie jogged out of his neighborhood and sprinted toward downtown. Within minutes he was in the heart of the Midgard II business district.

He passed stores, offices, arcades, and malls. He passed the Midgard High School, which was closed for the summer, and City Hall.

The soft ground he was running on hid the machines that kept Midgard II afloat. Vast engines and thrusters were buried in the core of the station.

The Midgard II was as organic as it was mechanical. The machines that powered the space station were built first, then the rest of the station was created and grown around the engine.

The makeup of the Midgard II fascinated Hobie. He had a keen interest in science. Hobie wanted to be a professional space explorer. To do so,

he had to first attend the science academy. That was fine with Hobie. He could hardly wait to apply.

His thoughts were interrupted at a downtown intersection when four vehicles blocked him from the crossing the street.

The vehicles were Skyyes, small spacecraft capable of travel on Midgard II and travel beyond the space station. Skyyes were the rage with the space station's teenagers. Hobie was eager to own one himself some day.

Hobie recognized the group that piled out of the Skyyes immediately. It was Simon Wrest and his friends, known as the Red Jumpers.

Simon ran a gloved hand through his blonde hair and smiled at Hobie. "Well, if it isn't 'Space Ace, Jr.', the Wonder Boy. How are you, Hobie?"

"I was fine till just a minute ago," Hobie sneered. In all the years they had

known each other, Hobie and Simon had never gotten along.

"Funny guy," Simon replied. "The boys and I are going to go warping. Want to join us?"

"You know I don't have a Skyye," Hobie said.

"Too bad. We're going through the red zones," Simon said, glancing back at the seven boys that made up his gang. "The blue zones are lame. They're for 'fraidy cats . . . like you."

"I don't have time for this," Hobie said, coolly turning away from the group.

"When you finally decide to grow up and leave your virtual reality games at home, look me up, Hobie," Simon called after him. The other Red Jumpers jeered in agreement.

Hobie tried not to care. "Only fools warp through dangerous red zones," he thought to himself.

Hobie looked at his watch and saw it was time for him to return home. As he rounded his block, sweaty from the run, he noticed his mother and father standing outside their home.

And then he noticed the brand new blue Skyye parked in front of their driveway!

CHAPTER 2

"Wow! Hey, Dad, is that for me?" Hobie asked, staring with disbelief at the Skyye.

"It sure is," Ernie Negron replied, smiling brightly. "I discussed it with your mother last night, and we agreed that it was time for you to have one."

"Surprise!" Carmen said with a smile. She had certainly fooled Hobie at lunch with her talk of refusing to get him a Skyye.

Hobie ran his hands down the sleek hood of the vehicle. "It's the greatest present I've ever gotten," he said, already anxious to hop into the cockpit.

"Well, before you take on the universe, there are a few things we need to discuss," said Carmen.

"Like what?" Hobie asked.

"The Skyyes are only for travel on Midgard II and in the blue zones," his mother replied.

"Of course," Hobie agreed. The blue zones were areas deemed safe by exploration teams. Red zones were dangerous, hostile areas that certain reckless youths, like Simon Wrest and his bunch, liked to travel through.

"We know you're a smart kid," Ernie chimed in. "But we also know what peer pressure is like. You have to promise us that you will never take your Skyye through a restricted red zone."

"I promise," Hobie assured them. "Besides, don't most Skyyes have built-in controls that prevent them from traveling through red zones?"

"Yes, but they can be turned off,"

Carmen said with a knowing look. "Especially by a bright kid with a lot of scientific skill. Do you know who I'm talking about?"

"Don't worry, Mom. I won't turn off the inhibitors," Hobie replied.

"Just see that you don't," Carmen said. Her expression became sad. "I don't want you lost in a red zone like we lost your brother Jack."

"That won't happen, Mom," Hobie reassured her. "And don't despair about Jack. His exploration ship had a suspended animation tube. If he crashed, I'm sure he got in the tube to keep himself safe till a search team finds him."

"And I'm sure they will," said Hobie's father. "Anyway, Hobie, we realized we were holding you back because of Jack's disappearance. That's why we decided to surprise you this way."

"Come in for some coffee before you have to go back to work, Ernie," Carmen said to her husband.

"I'll be right there," Ernie replied. "I want to give Hobie a few pointers, first."

Carmen nodded and went inside.

Ernie inspected the Skyye. "It sure is a beauty," Ernie said. "Do you think you can handle it okay?"

"You bet," Hobie said. "I've had lots of

practice with the virtual reality machine."

"Your brother was good at handling crafts, too . . . until he flew into that warp world in a red zone," Ernie said grimly.

"I know," Hobie said sadly. He remembered the day several months ago when Jack's field marshall had told the Negrons of Jack's disappearance. All

the known warp worlds were numbered. The marshall thought Jack had vanished into Warp World 3030.

"I've seen some pretty rough things firsthand out there, and there's no need for you to face them, too," Ernie said.

Hobie leaned against the hood of the Skyye, eager to hear what his father had to say about red zones.

"The red zones are filled with plenty of pitfalls, like Warp World 3030," continued Ernie. "The warp worlds are caught in some weird, dimensional flux. They go in and out of our reality constantly. One day, a whole planet might be in a certain sector of a red zone, and the next day it will be gone," Ernie said.

"Destroyed?" Hobie asked.

"No. It will just fade in and out of reality as we see it. We have no explanation for it yet. Some warp worlds fade out and are never seen again for months, sometimes years. And you never want to be in a red-zone sector that winks."

"What does that mean?" Hobie asked.

"Wink is a term we use for implosions," Ernie explained, "which means a sector folds over itself and literally ceases to be. The New Frontier, which we're exploring now, is a constantly changing galaxy. There are warp dimension pockets here, that are created and destroyed sometimes in minutes. We never explore an area until we are sure that it won't disappear altogether. You follow me?"

"Yes," Hobie said. "And don't worry. I'll never enter a red zone."

"Good," Ernie said. "Your brother Jack was exploring a red zone on an authorized mission. But the dimensional pocket winked before he could get out. You can't guess with these things, son."

"I know, Dad," Hobie insisted. "And I know Jack will turn up. There's always the chance that whatever dimensional pocket he went into will open again."

"I hope so, son," Ernie said. Hobie's father turned and headed back toward the Negron home.

"Alone at last!" Hobie thought, opening the Skyye hatch and climbing inside.

CHAPTER 3

Hobie set the Skyye instruments on hover mode and began a slow climb toward the Midgard II's upper atmosphere. He had practiced in enough virtual reality Skyye simulations to know precisely how to drive a real one.

When he reached a certain height, the field surrounding the station would open up and allow Hobie to pass into the void of space. All authorized space vehicles gave off a frequency, or electric pulse. This opened a space large enough for the crafts to pass through.

Hobie checked his instruments, then

glanced down at Midgard II. Everything looked so small. The readings on the console were stable, so Hobie passed through the field into the vacuum of space.

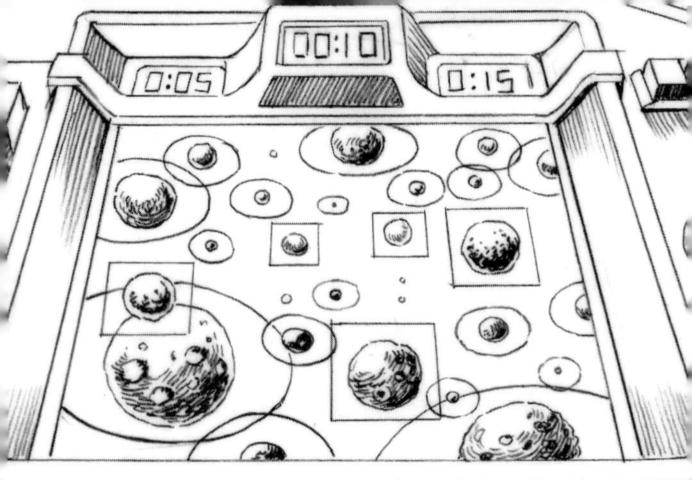

It was the most incredible moment of his life. Finally, he would know the thrill of space exploration. He turned on the thrusters and shot away from the Midgard II.

Instantly, a three-dimensional hologram screen lit up on the console. It showed the various zones of the galaxy in red and blue markings.

There were fourteen planets in this sector, five of which were in the blue zones. Hobie frowned at the large number of forbidden red zones on the

Skyye's console screen.

Red zones weren't just limited to the planets. There were dimensional pockets, black holes, and other galactic activity that he was not allowed to warp through.

Hobie set a course for the first planet in the blue zone, known simply as Planet 1. The console reading told him he would arrive in fifteen minutes.

Hobie could have cut that time by turning on his warp engine, but he wasn't in a rush to get there. On the way, he decided to pull from the computer all available data about the planet. The computer reported that Planet 1 was a planet which consisted mostly of water. It had a large population of marine life, but no land life whatsoever.

Hobie decided to go to the planet anyway and take some up-close atmospheric readings. He would stick to space observation from his Skyye. When Hobie was a little more experienced, he could land on the planets for first-hand observations.

Soon Hobie was close to the planet. He was sure to maintain a safe distance from its gravitational pull. He knew he could handle the Skyye if he were to enter Planet 1's atmosphere.

Hobie swept the surface of the planet with a scan ray and studied the atmosphere results on the computer.

The oxygen level of Planet 1 was too low for any human to breathe there without air tanks. Hobie turned the scan to the planet's ocean and produced images of the sea life.

The sea creatures were huge. The planet seemed to be populated by a large whale-like species. The computer reported that the creatures were of unknown origin.

That was the downside to exploration

work. Many things in the New Frontier galaxy were beyond human description. Until all the data could be input into the computer, only an incomplete reading of data would appear.

It was up to the exploration teams to discover the data the computer needed to solve the mysteries of the galaxy.

Hobie had learned from his mother that his scientific knowledge would not always apply to the unknown. There were whole new sciences to learn, new

wonders to behold. He was ready.

Hobie had turned his attention away from Planet 1 when he noticed a strange reading on his instruments. It came from a red zone in sector 13.

A dimensional pocket had opened and a planet was giving off a strange electromagnetic pulse.

It was hard to analyze because the pocket was beginning to fade. Hobie could now see what his father meant about the dangers of red zones.

Was the planet beyond the pocket in danger of winking? Hobie wasn't sure. He looked closely at his monitor and saw for the first time one of the biggest mysteries the crew of the Midgard II had discovered.

The dimensional pocket was like a hole in the fabric of reality. It was a door that had been opened to a different level of existence.

Hobie's mother once said that a pocket was like a mistake. It was a hole in space and when it faded it meant that the hole was mending itself.

Hobie studied the strange readings from the planet in the dimensional pocket for several minutes. But, unable to come to any conclusions, he finally gave up on the task.

Turning the scanning devices off, Hobie noticed other Skyyes were

warping in the same sector he was in.

"Good idea," he thought, eager to fire up his warp speed engine.

He turned the Skyye's automatic navigation system on. No one ever warped with manual control. The computer could route around all obstacles, including ones that the human eye would not see at warp speed until it was too late.

Hobie turned the Skyye in the direction of the Midgard II and switched on warp speed. Everything around him turned into a blur as the Skyye lurched into warp drive. It was dizzying.

Hobie glanced down at the monitor and could see the on-board computer mapping a clear path to the space station.

Within two minutes, he was orbiting the station.

Hobie checked the instruments for any possible problems. Everything checked out fine. He had made his first jump at light speed.

Hobie glanced down at the Midgard II. His home seemed so far away, and yet he knew he would be parked at his house within fifteen minutes.

From a distance, the station was just a small speck that revolved around the brilliant sun of the New Frontier.

Closer up, the station looked like a huge blue ball. Patterned after Earth, the station was a slightly scaled-down version of the home planet of Hobie's parents.

Hobie glanced to the empty

passenger's seat of the Skyye. "It would be great to share this experience with someone," he thought. "Who would be the perfect person to bring into the blue zone?"

He steered into the atmosphere of the Midgard II and began his descent.

CHAPTER 4

Hobie parked his Skyye outside the home of Ruby Escobar and her parents. He had grown up with Ruby and considered her his best friend.

There were times when Hobie wanted to be more than friends with Ruby. But it was hard to tell Ruby how he felt. She knew him so well that he was afraid it would ruin their friendship if they started dating.

Hobie walked gingerly up the path to the Escobar home and rang the bell.

Ruby answered the door. Her dark eyes brightened when she saw Hobie.

"Hi, Hobie," she said, brushing her

thick brown hair out of her eyes. "I haven't seen you in a couple of days."

"I've been running the Valhalla 7 program at home. It's taken up most of my time," Hobie said.

"What level have you reached?" Ruby asked.

"Ninth," Hobie replied.

"Well, I'm on the eleventh," Ruby bragged with a little smile. "What do you think of that?"

"You're cheating," Hobie kidded.

"Ha," Ruby smirked. "I'll be through with the program before you reach the tenth level."

"Don't be so sure," Hobie replied. He always enjoyed his friendly competition with Ruby.

"So, don't just stand there. Come in," Ruby said.

"Actually, can you come out for a second?" Hobie asked. "There's something I want to show you."

"Sure," Ruby replied, stepping out onto the front porch.

She followed Hobie to the driveway, then gasped in amazement when she saw the Skyye.

"Is this yours?" she asked, admiring the vehicle.

"Sure is," Hobie said. "Mom and Dad

gave it to me this afternoon."

"It's great!" Ruby said. "You must take me for a ride, right now!"

"Your wish is my command," Hobie said, opening the hatch to the Skyye so Ruby could enter.

Once seated inside, Hobie took the Skyye up and toward space. Hobie took Ruby warping through several sectors, relishing her excitement.

He navigated to Planet 1, explaining his readings to Ruby.

"I'll show you something interesting," Hobie said, turning his scan probe toward sector 13's red zone.

He explained the strange pulse in the planet's electromagnetic field.

"What could it be?" Ruby asked.

"I don't know," Hobie replied. "I'd like to find out."

"Why don't we?" Ruby said.

"We can't warp through a red zone," Hobie said. "It's against regulations."

"People do it all the time," Ruby said. "It's fun."

"It's very dangerous," Hobie maintained.

"Are you trying to tell me that you're not even the least bit curious?" Ruby asked. "I know that scientific mind of yours."

"I admit I'm curious," replied Hobie. "But when I go into a red zone, I want it to be as part of an exploration team."

"Don't tell me you're scared," Ruby teased her friend.

"Ruby, my parents have already lost one son to a red zone. I don't think they could handle going through that again. Now, if that makes me a loser in Simon Wrest's eyes or a coward in yours, I'm sorry," Hobie said angrily.

"No, I'm sorry," Ruby said. She looked down at her feet then back at Hobie. "Maybe we should head back."

"I think that's a good idea," Hobie muttered.

Hobie knew he had promised his parents that he wouldn't explore the red zones alone. But deep down he knew he wanted to. He wanted to prove to Simon and Ruby that he wasn't afraid.

CHAPTER 5

"Truce," Ruby declared with a hopeful smile as Hobie hovered the Skyye over the main strip of the Midgard II.

"Okay," Hobie said, shaking Ruby's outstretched hand. He couldn't stay mad at her for too long.

"Why don't we go to the arcade?" Ruby suggested. "I haven't played skeetball in a long time."

"Sure," Hobie said, bringing the Skyye down.

He parked at the curb of the main complex. As he and Ruby stepped out onto the sidewalk, he noticed Simon Wrest. Simon gazed with approval at

ARCADE

Hobie's new Skyye.

"Nice ride," Simon said.

"Thanks," Hobie replied, noticing the rest of the Red Jumpers piling out of the arcade.

"You got it just in time for an initiation," Simon said.

"What are you talking about?" Hobie asked slowly.

"We noticed a dimensional pocket on our Skyye instruments while we were warping earlier," Simon explained.

"You mean the one in sector 13?" Hobie asked.

"You monitored it, too? Maybe there's hope for you yet," Simon replied.

"I wouldn't try to reach the planet through the hole," Hobie warned. "It's fading. And there's a really weird signal coming from the planet's electromagnetic field."

"Everybody always freaks out about fading dimensions," Simon protested.

"Your average dimension fade will reappear in one or two days."

"But some never appear again," Hobie argued. "Besides, I don't want to be stuck in a hostile dimension on a hostile planet for an hour, much less a day."

"Where's your sense of adventure?" Simon asked. "There's a brave new galaxy to explore and you'd rather stay here on this floating heap and play skeetball."

"This brave new galaxy you're talking about has too many unstable zones," Hobie replied.

"You really disappoint me, Hobie," Simon said, shaking his head. "I always thought you were pretty cool, but . . ."

"Simon, you know we've never gotten along," Hobie interrupted.

"For obvious reasons," Simon said, smiling at Ruby. "But I can't believe the son of Ernie 'Space Ace' Negron won't warp a red zone."

"Leave him alone, Simon," Ruby cut in. "He has his reasons."

Hobie felt himself growing angry again. He didn't want to explain himself to Simon. He could outwarp Simon and the Red Jumpers any day. He had nothing to prove to them.

"I'm out of here," Hobie announced. "Are you coming, Ruby?"

Ruby shook her head, avoiding Hobie's eyes for a moment. "Hobie, I'm

going with Simon through the red zone. I have to see it."

"All right!" Simon grinned. "I think we have a new Red Jumper here."

"Do you know what you could be getting into, Ruby?" Hobie asked.

"No, I don't, to tell you the truth," said Ruby. "But I've got to check it out. Sorry, Hobie."

"Fine," Hobie said, opening the hatch

to his Skyye. "If you want to go with these guys, fine. I only hope I see you again," he snarled.

"If you change your mind, we'll be taking off in an hour," Simon said. "That is, if you find any guts between now and then."

Hobie closed the hatch to the jeers of the Red Jumpers and headed home.

CHAPTER 6

Hobie sat at the computer in his bedroom. He ran an analysis on the electromagnetic field from the unknown planet of sector 13.

There were no new answers.

He had a feeling that he was missing something, but he couldn't put his finger on it. Hobie headed back to the arcade.

He was intent on talking the Red Jumpers out of warping into sector 13. Maybe Simon would listen to reason this time. Hobie had been too angry before. Now, his concern for Ruby was overshadowing his anger.

When he arrived at the arcade, Hobie saw the Red Jumpers gathered in the driveway. As he parked his Skyye, Hobie noticed that Simon's Skyye was missing.

He walked up to Isaac Frazier. Isaac was Simon's right-hand man. He looked a little pale and clearly nervous about something.

"Where are Simon and Ruby?" Hobie asked.

"They jetted into sector 13," Isaac said. "The rest of us decided not to go. After hearing you and checking out sector 13 myself, I realized how dangerous it was."

"And they went anyway?" Hobie asked with concern.

Isaac nodded grimly. "They warped in fine, then things got weird."

"What happened?" Hobie prodded.

Isaac shook his head. "As soon as they pierced the dimensional hole and warped to the atmosphere of that planet, their readings began to fade."

"Fade?" Hobie asked, fear rising up inside of him.

"Yeah, it was like the planet sucked the energy out of his Skyye," Isaac said.

"Of course!" Hobie realized. "I should have figured it out before."

"Figured what out?" Isaac asked.

"There's no time to explain," Hobie said. "I need the power modules from your Skyyes."

"Why?" Issac asked. "Shouldn't we get help, instead?"

"There's no time," Hobie explained. "That sector could go at any minute. I think it's a warp world. I'm going to take the red zone inhibitor off my Skyye. Have those power modules ready by the time I'm through."

Moments later, Hobie was ready to fly. "Call for help," Hobie told Isaac. "Call my parents at work."

Hobie took off, not knowing exactly

what to expect in sector 13. But he had a plan–he just hoped it would work!.

Hobie warped out of the Midgard II atmosphere. His console was already displaying the field that he now thought

was a power-dampening field.

If Hobie's theory was right, Simon's Skyye had travelled too close to the planet and the Skyye's power module had been drained.

All Hobie had to do was come up with the proper frequency that would disrupt the field long enough for him to get a new module to Simon.

But Ruby was his main worry. He admitted to himself that he had been jealous when she decided to warp with Simon. But now her safety was his only concern.

As Hobie approached the dimensional pocket of sector 13, he was amazed at the brilliant light shining from the hole in space.

It looked like eternity, a peephole opening up to reveal greater possibilities. He just hoped he lived long enough to retell the experience to his parents.

KYYE

Hobie entered the opening.

He shut off the warp engines and kicked in the thrusters. He found a low-level pitch he thought would stop the power-dampening field.

His monitor showed a meteor belt in the distance. "No problem," he thought, switching on the autopilot. The computer would plot a course through the field.

Hobie started making a rescue plan as the Skyye began to manuever through the field. Suddenly, he felt a weight press down on the Skyye. He looked up from the monitor, straight into a single red, searing eye.

A huge, reptilian space creature with a wingspan twice the size of the Skyye had latched onto the ship.

Hobie watched in horror as the beast began to squeeze the cockpit in its enormous claws!

CHAPTER 7

Hobie quickly switched off the autopilot and grabbed the controls. He had to try shaking the monster off before it cracked open the Skyye like a brittle eggshell.

He also had to dodge the path of free-floating meteors. He increased his speed, but the monster clung on.

The only option left to Hobie was a series of spins and turns in the shower that he hoped would shake the creature off the Skyye.

Hobie jerked the controls. The Skyye did a somersault, spinning between two meteors. The creature was scraped off

the Skyye and Hobie could hear its shriek as it fell away.

"Didn't anyone ever tell you that hitch-hiking was dangerous?" Hobie smiled as he slowed to normal speed. He then reset the autopilot.

He wiped the sweat from his

forehead. "That was too close," he said.

Finally, Hobie cleared the meteor shower and saw the planet in the distance. It was a bright red orb that pulsed with energy.

Hobie did a quick scan and discovered the atmosphere was barely breathable for humans, although no plant life seemed to grow there.

Another mystery: What created the oxygen? Without trees, there should be no oxygen. Hobie did a closer analysis. He discovered the atmosphere itself was similiar to oxygen.

But Hobie's research could wait until he and the others were safely back home. He slowed his engines and began bombarding the planet's field with the frequency he hoped would break up the dampening pulse.

After a few moments, the pulse began to weaken. Hobie began his descent to the planet.

The landscape was flat and barren. Hobie received a faint reading from Simon's Skyye. He followed it, hovering hundreds of feet over the red sand of the desert planet.

Though there were no visual signs of life, Hobie's scan was picking up life-forms everywhere. This bothered him. Maybe there was an underground civilization. His thoughts on the matter were interrupted when he finally came across Simon's Skyye.

Simon and Ruby were standing beyond it, scouring the remains of a crashed exploration ship. The twisted hunk of metal looked like a part of the landscape. They waved their arms furiously at Hobie.

Hobie checked his instruments. The disruptor was still holding against the dampening field, so he landed.

After setting down, Hobie leapt out of the Skyye. Ruby and Simon rushed up to him.

"My Skyye is sapped," Simon said, his face fearful and unsure. "It took the last bit of power I had to land. Plus, the oxygen level's low here. I can feel my own energy sapping."

Ruby brushed past Simon and grabbed Hobie's arm. "Come over here, Hobie."

Ruby led him to the charred remains of the ship that Simon had parked his Skyye beside.

As they entered the ship, Hobie realized that it looked like an exploration ship. Could it be?

Ruby led him to the dimly lit bridge of the small ship. Right in front of them was Jack Negron. He was motionless, locked in the suspended animation tube.

Hobie's brother had crashed here, and must have entered the tube to survive until he was found!

"Let's get him out and head home before our energy is sapped by the low oxygen level. We also have the pocket to worry about getting through," Hobie said.

He quickly shut off the controls. Then he lifted the glass lid up and pulled Jack out of the tube.

Jack' s eyelids fluttered, and he tried to speak.

Hobie knew that it would take Jack awhile to clear his head. Hobie and

Ruby wrapped Jack's arms around their shoulders and left the craft.

"How do we get out of here?" Simon asked in a panic.

"With these," Hobie said, handing Simon a power module. "I've managed to weaken the field that caused your Skyye to lose power. Fire it up and I'll set the frequency on your instruments to keep the hole in the field open."

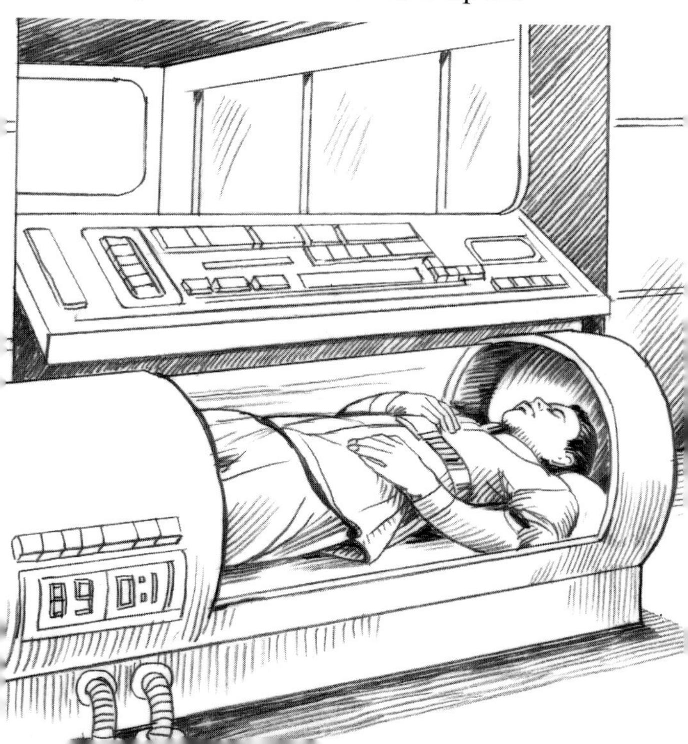

Simon nodded and the trio went to Simon's ship. Simon snapped in the module. Hobie strapped Jack into the passenger side of Simon's Skyye.

The Skyye powered up. Hobie quickly adjusted the frequency.

"Hobie!" Ruby screamed.

Hobie ducked out of the Skyye in

time to witness the soil of the planet begin to move.

Scaly creatures that seemed to grow out of the soil arose everywhere Hobie looked.

The red sand creatures opened yellow, sunken eyes. Their mouths bared hooked fangs. Three creatures sprang at Simon and clutched at him. Simon screamed and tried to fight them off. Hobie and Ruby ran to him and pulled two of the creatures away. Simon freed himself from the third.

"Get into your ship and take off!" Hobie commanded. "Get my brother back to Midgard II!"

Simon climbed into the Skyye.

"We've got to get to my Skyye!" Hobie shouted to Ruby while fending the creatures off.

"There are too many of them!" Ruby shouted back.

There was no time for argument.

Simon rocketed away as Hobie and Ruby fought off the creatures and finally made their way to Hobie's Skyye.

They jumped into the ship, slamming the hatch above them. The creatures were swarming all over the craft.

"The frequency I created must have awakened them," Hobie said.

"There's no time for figuring it out, Hobie!" Ruby cried. "Let's just get out of here, fast!"

The creatures began to rock the ship. Hobie revved his thrusters. It was enough to shake them off. The Skyye rose into the air.

"It should be smooth sailing from here," Hobie assured Ruby.

But just then a warning light showed up on his monitor. The dimensional pocket was fading.

The whole sector was about to wink out of existence!

CHAPTER 8

Hobie's Skyye rose through the atmosphere and into space.

"We may be in trouble, Ruby," Hobie reported.

Ruby glanced at the instruments. "Are we going to make it out before the sector winks?"

"Hang on," Hobie said. He switched on the warp drive.

Hobie scanned the planet they had just left. It was coming apart at the seams. Stars were burning out all around them and the planet was now a cloud of gas.

Hobie monitored the destruction on

his console. Everything behind them was being devoured.

Hobie noticed that they were approaching the hole again. They had only seconds to make it, or they'd be swallowed up in the eye of the storm.

A white, blinding light filled the void of space. Hobie shielded his eyes. "We're not going to make it," he thought.

Suddenly, the light died down.

Hobie stared up through the cockpit.

Several emergency crafts were stationed around the brink of the spot where the hole had been minutes ago.

"Are you all right?" a concerned voice asked over the Skyye communicator.

Hobie glanced over at Ruby. Her face reflected the relief he felt.

"We're fine," Hobie replied. "Just fine." Ruby smiled at him and nodded.

The emergency team escorted Hobie's Skyye back to the station.

A crowd was waiting for Hobie and Ruby on the main street of downtown Midgard II.

Hobie landed his Skyye. He and Ruby stepped out to a greeting of cheers from a crowd of people.

His parents were standing in front. Jack stood with them, though he still looked dazed.

"You're a hero, son," said Ernie Negron as he reached out to give Hobie a hug. "I couldn't have done a better job myself. You've got what it takes!"

"I was so worried about you. Don't you ever go into a red zone again," Carmen Negron warned, holding Hobie in a tight embrace.

"He won't have to worry about that."

Hobie turned to see Simon Wrest and the Red Jumpers gathered around him.

"The Red Jumpers are disbanding," Simon continued. "You were right. It's too dangerous to warp through unchartered territory."

Simon offered Hobie his hand.

"I want to apologize for always giving you such a hard time," he said.

Hobie shook Simon's hand. "It's okay, Simon. I'm just glad I could help you out."

"That was a fine job, Hobie," Jack said, ruffling Hobie's dark locks. Hobie was overjoyed to see his brother. Jack was going to be all right now.

"That's because he takes after me,"

Carmen said with a smile.

"You should apply at the science academy after high school and join the space explorers," Jack suggested. "You saved my life, little brother."

Jack shook Hobie's hand, too.

"That's what brothers are for," Hobie said. He turned to Ruby, whose smile spoke for her. Then his eyes traveled upward into the darkening sky. What other adventures awaited him out there? He didn't know.

But Hobie Negron was ready.